THE JOURNEY OF GETTING
THE GIRL OF MY DREAMS
An ordinary man,
an extraordinary journey of love.

THE JOURNEY OF GETTING
THE GIRL OF MY DREAMS
An ordinary man,
an extraordinary journey of love.

Rohit Chawhan

ZORBA BOOKS

ZORBA BOOKS

Published in India by Zorba Books, 2017

Website: www.zorbabooks.com
Email: info@zorbabooks.com

ISBN Print Book - 978-93-86407-65-8
ISBN eBook - 978-93-86407-66-5

Zorba Books Pvt. Ltd.(opc)
Gurgaon, INDIA

Printed at Repro Knowledgecast Limited, Thane

Dedicated to

ALL PEOPLE WHO DARE TO LOVE

My thanks to Rupali Gohil, Sadique Ali Hashmi, Abhinav Janghel, Amitoj Singh and Vinod Chawhan for inspiring and supporting me.

I also want to thank the people whom I have never met but love

Kriti Sanon, Sharukh Khan and Sandeep Maheshwari

FOREWORD

I am delighted to write the foreword for this incredible love story by Rohit Chawhan. I met Rohit in Durg last year, where I was delivering an inspirational talk on my life and how I was able to climb the corporate ladder and I had no idea that will inspire Rohit to pursue his dream of becoming a writer at such a young age and the subsequent respect he has bestowed on me with this honour of writing a foreword for this book.

It is a beautiful story of love juxtaposed with the journey of our lives. It is captivating from the word go and continues to inspire each one of us to pursue our passions and never give up in spite of all the challenges that we face. It is a story of how experiencing love can make your heart race and allow you to achieve impossible things. It is a story of positive self-belief which can be directed towards gaining the respect and love of your loved one, even though the odds are heavily stacked against you. You will be known for the excellence you have pursued and the impact you have had on lives, not by the colour of your skin or your physical appearance.

In my life I have faced several challenges and the spirit of 'Never say Die' and 'Never lose Hope' has allowed me to achieve success beyond my dreams and this is exactly what this book continues to unfold chapter after chapter as it impels you to reflect on your own personal journey of love. You want Ashish the main character to persevere and not give up on his passion even after leaving home as his parents could not understand him and were not willing to support his dreams.

When you love someone and get no reciprocity, it breaks one's heart and it seems crazy to continue to pursue a lost cause, but this story is about hope, heartbreak and love. It will re-create your world of love and bring excitement and that tingling feeling in your knees. How love makes you transform yourself and how miracles can happen.

So sit back, get entertained and believe that it is possible to conquer all odds and enjoy the roller coaster. It is remarkable that this is Rohit's first book. I am sure he will go on to weave many stories which will continue to give us a happy feeling and courage to follow our passions and continue to dream big and most importantly love.

Tarun Anand
Former MD, South Asia of Thomson Reuters
Founder of Universal Business School

PREFACE

Love is just a word until you find someone who gives it a definition.

It has different meanings for different people. For some, love may mean to chill, for others, it's a time pass, while there are many who still believe that it is the reason for them to wake up every morning.

This story is about Ashish and Kriti.

All relations are created by blood, but some are created by love. The bond of love is so beautiful that it cannot be described or told in words. But is it always easy to find love?

I don't call myself a professor of love, but the answer is a big 'no'.

The journey of finding the perfect Mr or Mrs is not an easy one, but it is an interesting one.

BEAUTY IS NOT IN THE FACE BUT IN THE HEART.
LOVE ISN'T EASY but IT'S WORTH IT.

CONTENTS

1. The Day That Chaged My Life   1

2. Problems and Solutions   6

3. One-Sided Love   20

4. Workout   27

5. Love Is Great   34

6. The Break Up   42

7. Miracles Do Happen   51

Epilogue   69

Epilogue by Anurag Batra   71

Worksheet   73

CHAPTER 1

THE DAY THAT CHANGED MY LIFE

It was a sunny Sunday morning as I reached the airport to catch my flight to New York. After checking in, I had just picked up a cup of coffee from Starbucks when I noticed a very well-dressed handsome man. He was in a jet black suit with a pink tie and dark brown shoes.

The first thought that came to my mind was that he was a corporate dude travelling on business.

I went through security and was welcomed into the aircraft by an attractive stewardess who pointed me to my seat. I was hoping that I would get an interesting co-passenger next to me. And lo and behold, who do I get beside me? It was the very person I was admiring a few minutes ago!

He greeted me with a smile and I smiled back. I kept silent for a while controlling my excitement. Soon, the flight took off and I decided to introduce myself.

"Hello! I'm Rohit Chawhan," I proffered my hand. "Hi! I'm Ashish." He shook my hand.

"So Ashish, what do you do?"

"Well, I'm a chef, writer, businessman…all in one!"

"Sounds interesting! Lovely to meet you," I said genuinely.

"What do you do?" he asked.

"Nothing!"

"Sorry?"

I laughed and said, "Actually, I'm a student."

"Aah ok," he smiled. "Well, I'm going to NY for the opening of my new restaurant."

"Wow! Congratulations! I'm just going for a holiday and to meet my relatives."

"Good for you," he responded.

I couldn't contain my curiosity so I just asked. "So is this your family business?"

"No no…I am a self-made man. It's all my own!"

"Great! Do you have a girlfriend?"

"Girlfriend? No girlfriend, but a wife – and she's enough to kill a man with her looks! Only after meeting her I realised that beauty and brains do co-exist," he said with a twinkle in his eye.

"So where did you meet her?"

"It's a long story…are you really up for it?"

"Well, it's a long journey from Mumbai to NY too – I'm listening," I said laughing.

"This is the first time someone's ever asked – so here goes…buckle up and be ready to hear how I got the girl of my dreams.

"I was 17 and in 12th grade – the stage of life when you are fearless. It was the last day of my mid-term exams. It was Math and the paper was tough and I knew I hadn't done well. I was in a terrible mood when I came back home and although I told my mother that I had done well, it was a lie. I quickly ate my lunch and retired to my room for a nap.

"I woke up just on time for my coaching class and rushed out. Just as I parked my scooty and was entering my class, I saw this tall and slim girl wearing a grey shirt and well-fitted blue jeans! I have rewound that magical scene in my head at least a thousand times!

"I couldn't take my eyes off Kriti. She had light pink lips, beautiful blue eyes and long black hair. I was mesmerised. She was what I had dreamt off. She passed me by without noticing me. I had already fallen madly in love with her. It was love at first sight!

'I could not concentrate in class that day. I kept thinking of her all through the class. I had never seen her in class before so I asked my friend who she was.

She was a 2nd year student who was doing her designing course and her name was kriti. Her name sounds as beautiful as she looks, I said dreamily.

3

'Well, she's older than you, so chill,' said my friend, 'be happy with 60s and 70s songs.'

"I spent the next few days thinking of how to approach her. After a few days, I got my chance. There was a test and we were made to sit with the 2nd year students. I was overjoyed when I saw that I would be sitting beside Kriti! It was destiny – or else how could one explain the coincidence of me getting to sit right beside Kriti?

"I couldn't believe that I was actually sitting near her. I could see the other boys looking at me enviously and felt even luckier.

"All through the test, I was conscious of her sitting right there and kept looking up to look at her. At one point, she caught my eye and asked me what my name was.

'Ashish, can you help me please?' she asked in very low voice. I nodded enthusiastically wanting to do anything she asked.

'Okay then can you please pass me the paper the person sitting in front is holding out?'

"I took the paper from the person and gave it to her. Our hands touched and I felt as though I got an electric shock! The test got over and yes, I failed again – but this time it was not because I hadn't prepared well for it, it was because I was too distracted to actually even write anything!

"When my teacher saw my blank paper, he slapped me hard right across my face and reprimanded me, 'Is this what you want your future to be? You have done nothing and will do nothing in life.'

"I left the class dejected, forcing back the tears threatening to roll down my face. More than anything else, it was so embarrassing to be slapped and yelled at like that. I knew my life was not going anywhere and this humiliation made it even worse. My friend Abhinav consoled me by telling me that there would be many more exams in life but beautiful moments like the ones I had experienced would be few and far between. Hence I should savour those moments and not feel bad about them.

"I took a few days off from coaching. When I finally started going back, I looked around for Kriti but she was nowhere to be seen. I asked one of my friends if they knew why she had not been coming only to be told that she had gone off to Germany for further studies.

"I left the coaching centre and started driving around with no idea of where to go or what to do. I finally went back home and slept. I felt I had lost my reason to live. But I woke up the next day determined not to quit. I was sure that sooner or later my problems would get solved.

As Steve Jobs said, have the courage to follow your passion.

So I did."

CHAPTER 2

THE PROBLEM AND SOLUTIONS

"So you were not good in studies...and she left too," I mused as Ashish looked down at his hands. I continued, "So what did you do after that?"

He took a deep breath and said, "Chef. I wanted to become a chef. It was difficult to convince my parents that a chef too can have a good life...but I did manage to do that finally."

"That's an unusual choice of career," I commented.

"Yes, but I persisted. I did what I really wanted to and that's how I am able to travel business class...that's how I have an opening of a restaurant in another country today."

"Just do what you love and you will get whatever you want in life," said Ashish looking straight into my eyes.

"You're a philosopher too! Great!" I said to him. "So sir, tell me what happened next..."

"Well, as I said, I wanted to be a chef...wanted to be known for my innovative cooking...wanted to have restaurants all over the world...I had big dreams. But the problem was that nobody believed in me or in my dreams. Everyone I knew had something or the other to say – you? A chef? Come on, think of something better to pursue... want to keep cutting vegetables in the kitchen all your life?? All those who were sceptical about my choice of profession now praise what I do!

"That's the thing with the world – if you are not successful no one will pay any attention to you. But if you are rich and successful, then whatever bullshit you say will be lapped up hungrily and followed too! That's the rule of the world.

"So although my parents forced me to study physics, chemistry and maths so that I could become an engineer, in my heart I always knew that I would do something different.

"The ultimate aim of making a child study hard is to get him into a good college so that he can get a good job thereafter. The idea is that he or she make money. Today, **there is no profession in the world in which you cannot earn money. You just need to choose the one you enjoy. The one that you are passionate about. Once you do that, your job ceases to be just a job, it becomes a passion. And that passion will make you the best in that field**. When it comes to respect, the more money you have, the more respect you will get!

"Personally, I do not believe that money is the most important thing in the world, but in the world, we live in, there is nothing that cannot be bought – everything has a price. You pay more, you get a better doctor, you pay more, you get better services. That's the rule of the world we live in," said Ashish emphatically.

"After she left, I had nothing to look forward to. I didn't feel like waking up in the morning, felt listless all day when I finally dragged myself out – I did not like my classes and was struggling. I couldn't talk to anyone – to me, they all seemed to be more bothered about making friends online and getting likes rather than listening to my sad stories. I got into depression and felt lousy about myself. There was no one in my family that I could speak with either. I immersed myself in trying hard to just pass my class 12 exams anyhow so that I could then choose what I wanted to really do. I managed to get an average score and then got admission into an average college in Mumbai.

"One day I gathered the guts to speak with my father. I went up to him and said that I wanted to talk with him. He gestured to me to sit down on the sofa in front of him. As I sat down nervously, my courage started to fail me. I swallowed hard and shook my head and started talking.

'There's a cooking course that I have found out about in America and it has turned out really great chefs. I have researched it well and I really want to go there,' I blurted out in one go.

"My father stared at me wondering what I was talking about when I continued, I really want to go Papa, please don't stop me."

'You actually want to go to college to learn cooking?' my father looked at me incredulously. 'Are you serious? Your mother and the other ladies can teach you all this if you want! Why spend so much money to go to another country to learn cooking?' he laughed out loud.

'I just want your permission and some money – I promise to repay you when I get a job. The rest I will manage on my own. Please say yes, Papa.'

"He stood up and called out to my mother. 'Did you hear what this good-for-nothing son of yours is asking me for?'

My mother nodded and said that she would explain things to me. 'Enough of explaining now – there will be no more talk of this cooking-*shuking* – Ashish, please focus on your engineering. You need to do an MBA after that.'

"I looked at him in surprise. It seemed that he hadn't heard a word of what I had been saying. When I finally said no, he slapped me hard across my face."

'What's wrong with you? I will pay for your studies and I know what's good for you. I know you better than you know yourself and I will decide your future.' I don't know how I got the courage, but I told him that there was no way he was going to decide my future.

"He was livid. But I was adamant too. I said, 'Dad, not this time. I have already wasted enough of my life doing what you have told me to – I hate it. Maybe I'm not cut out for engineering.'

'The argument carried on and on and he finally said, 'If you want to live here, then you have to follow my wishes...'

"It was then that I decided. I had to leave home to follow my dreams.

"And that's exactly what I did. 'So, since you will not support my dream, I do not need anything from you. I am leaving the house.

"And so I did. I left the house with my father's taunts haunting me – let's see how you manage your bills on your own from now.

"I was now even more adamant to succeed. I quit college and got myself a job at a restaurant. I had a little money saved up and I used that to get myself a small room to live in. It was very difficult to live in such a slum-like place but I had no choice. I couldn't afford anything else.

"My job at the restaurant earned me a salary of 9000 rupees per month. I had to work 14 hours from 9 in morning to 11 at night. There was nothing right or good. I had to take this step because I knew in my heart that this was way better than becoming and following a profession I hated. I knew that my parents just wished for me to have a good life but I couldn't afford to let my dreams die. They didn't believe in my dreams – they thought that becoming a chef was a waste of time. To them, there was no future in cooking. But I knew in my mind what I needed to do. So although 9000 rupees sounds quite grand, it was a meagre amount when I had to pay my rent of 4000 rupees. I would spend the rest on books and research about cooking and recipes. I spent a lot on my reading about Michelin chefs and their lives. I could hardly save anything but I needed to buy the books to prepare for my college admission.

"I was so passionate about learning more and more that I would finish a whole book in one night. I loved what I was doing but I also needed to improve my living conditions. I started sending my resumes to big hotels to take me on as a chef. I got a few calls and even went for interviews, but when they learnt where I was working or where I lived, they were like, come next time, but that next time never came.

"Being slightly dyslexic, I was very conscious of my disability and couldn't make too many friends. I had lost touch with most of my school friends when I left home but Sadique and Abhinav stood by me.

"Sadique was pursuing law from a national university and Abhinav was an event manager. Both were always available for me and always encouraged me. They never ever made fun of me, my looks (I was fat and being short made me look even worse), my disabilities or my choice of career. Whenever they could, they also helped me financially.

"It was a holiday and I had the day off too. We were all at this place near a bakery – it was our *adda* – a place we'd all meet and chat over endless cups of tea and cigarettes. Our discussions were mainly about beautiful girls, about whose girlfriend was the best and so on. Both Sadique and Abhinav had girlfriends so they didn't really say much, but I didn't and therefore, said whatever I had to!

"And so, that day we ended up talking about the studs who had the hottest girls…and how they'd swagger around doing all kinds of unmentionable things. I didn't think that anyone could become a stud by doing stupid stuff like this – to me, one is a stud only by his talent and how he works on it and of course, the way he meets and treats people.

"During the conversation, someone mentioned Kriti. My ears perked up – and I was like, 'that Kriti? That tall and beautiful one?' Abhinav nodded and asked why. I said nothing.

'Check out her profile pic – she looks awesome.' I rushed to get a Wi-Fi hotspot and logged on to Facebook. I searched for her name and there she was – she was looking gorgeous. Even better than she did earlier. I closed my eyes for a second to thank God for helping me find her again. It'd been ages that something nice had happened to me and I looked at it as a good omen.

"She looked even more beautiful than she had a year ago. Her smile was worth millions and her beautiful blue eyes, I swear, were enough to even make Hitler fall in love and follow the road to peace. I looked through her page and opened all her albums to see her pictures. I finally sent her a friend request.

"I started to believe in love from the first time I saw her.

"I lay awake that night checking Facebook every few minutes to see if she had accepted my request. Finally, I got the notification I was waiting for at 1 am. 'Kriti has accepted your request.' I was like yes, yes, yes, yes. I was ecstatic!

"I opened Facebook Messenger and sent her a message immediately. 'Hello, long time!' Her reply came within a couple of minutes. My heart was pounding hard as I wrote, 'Do you remember me?'

"Yes, came the reply almost immediately, 'Yes, of course, I remember you! Where are you these days?'

'Am here in Mumbai – where are you? What are you doing these days?'

'Hey, I'm in Mumbai too! I'm doing a designing course here. We should meet!'

"My heart leapt with joy when I read what she had written, but I controlled myself. 'But you'd gone to Germany, right? When did you get back?'

'Yes, I had gone to Germany – I went for a training for a couple of months, but now I'm back here in India. Imagine, we've both been in the same city and didn't even know that!'

'So what are you doing these days?' she asked.

"I didn't know what to say, I didn't want to tell her that I was a cook at a small restaurant. I panicked. Should I tell her the truth or tell a lie? But then something odd happened to me and I just couldn't bring myself to lie to her. I started saying that I was studying hotel management at a reputed college but then quickly changed track and said, 'I'm a chef.'

'Good for you! Pursuing what you want to do. That's great actually!'

"She didn't sound surprised. She was just so normal about the whole thing that I began to relax. We chatted for a while about this and that and finally, said bye after promising to meet up soon.

"That conversation with Kriti, not even a real conversation, but a cyber one, kept me going for the next 10 days. I was happy to have reconnected with her and was wondering how to take the next step. I had a habit of speaking to myself because I was alone most of the time. It helped me to internalise what I was thinking about and get a perspective on new things. It also helped me to get out of thinking depressive thoughts. I knew I had taken a very crucial decision of leaving home, and although I was determined to succeed, I felt that my life was a mess – I wanted to do more than make the usual food at the restaurant, I wanted to experiment. I also wanted a better place to live in. I wanted to have more fun but there was never enough money…I psyched myself every day saying that I would get out of this situation sooner than later.

"I was also determined to have a girlfriend now. I called both Sadique and Abhinav (who already had girlfriends) to please come over right away. They rushed to me, 'Is everything, okay bro? What happened? Are you okay?'

'I'm in love!'

'Seriously?' asked Abhinav incredulously. 'Not possible,' said Sadique looking at me disbelievingly. 'Come on Ashish, this is no time for jokes.'

'I'm fucking serious man, I'm really in love with someone!'

"I asked them to relax and put a kettle to boil. 'I'll tell you all. But wait, relax a bit, have some of my famous *chai*.'

"And then, just like a general walks in front of his battalion with his hands behind his back, I stood in front of them and looked at them seriously. 'Gentlemen, it's true that I am in love. I am serious. And I need your help. Please help me.'

"When they realized that I was really serious they stood up and hugged me in turn. 'Welcome to the club! But who's the girl?'

'Kriti.'

'Who Kriti?'

"I opened my phone and showed them Kriti's picture. They stared at the screen and then looked at each other and then at me again. Their mouths were wide open.

'So, what do you think?'

'Do you even know what're you talking about? You're mad!'

'Why? What?' I was shocked at their reaction.

"Abhinav hit me at the back of my head twice saying, 'Do you even know what the fuck you are saying? Do you even know who you're talking about? This is impossible.'

"I said nothing is impossible. I was really surprised at their reaction. I thought they would be happy for me and help me out, but all they both could say was, 'Shut up man, just shut the fuck up! You seriously called us here so urgently to tell us this bullshit? Really?'

'If you can't motivate me as friends, then just get out of my life,' I said rudely.

'Listen to me carefully Ashish. Listen to what I have to say and then you decide what you want to do, okay?'

'It's time to face reality. Kriti is someone that all the studs are after. Nobody's been able to get her. Second, she is too beautiful and smart for you! Yes seriously!'

"He picked up my notebook and started writing something in it while discussing with Sadique. 'Shut up and sit down for a while,' both Sadique and Abhinav said almost simultaneously. After a couple of minutes, they handed me the notebook back with some points written in it. They asked me to read it out aloud.

1. *She has everything and you have nothing.*

"When I tried to say something, they told me to shut up and continue reading. So I continued.

2. *She is beautiful and you are ugly.*

"I tried to say something again, but their looks made me stop and start reading again.

I continued to read.

3. *She is slim and you are fat.*

4. *She is tall and you are way shorter than her.*

5. *She is studying and you're not.*

6. *She is rich and moves around in that richie-rich circle – you have just Sadique and Abhinav as friends – neither of us is rich.*

7. *The most important thing is that she is 22 and you are 19.*

"I looked up at their expectant faces. I had plenty to say but was not being able to say any of it."

'Pursuing Kriti is not something that will give you happiness. In fact, you will fall flat on your face and become a laughing stock. It will leave you devastated. So it's better to focus on what you can do and stop daydreaming. This is an impossible task.'

'No brother, it is NOT impossible. And I will show it to you. I will prove you both wrong.'

'Well then, since you don't want to listen to us, do whatever you want. We still say it's impossible but if you want to still try, go ahead…we know what the results will be. If you need us, you know we'll be here…but for now, goodbye!' They stormed out of my house.

"I lay down on my bed as soon as they left. Heart of hearts, I knew they cared for me and that they were not wrong, but I wanted to try once at least. At least, I'll have the satisfaction of having tried.

"I put on my shoes to get some fresh air at the park I went to every evening. I enjoyed going there because not only did I get some fresh air and exercise, I also got to chat with a lot of the over-60 people who came to the park. They would look forward to interacting with me as much as I enjoyed chatting with them because they hardly had anyone to chat to. Everyone was too busy to give them anytime. They were just as lonely as I was and so we were perfect for each other. I was happy to see Robin Uncle – I loved talking to him. He understood me very well.

'What's the matter, young man? You have a glow on your face!'

'I'm in love!'

'That's great news! So who's the lucky girl?'

'Her name's Kriti. I've only met her a few times but I know that she is the girl of my dreams.'

'Do you have a picture of her?'

'Good choice! Your choice is just like your high ambitions!'

'Thank you very much, but am not sure that I will get her!'

'Hey, nothing is impossible if you try hard enough. Don't ever give up.'

"I nodded and showed him what my friends had written. He looked at it and was silent for some time. Then he took out his lighter and burnt the paper. I was aghast!

'A paper cannot teach you how to make a girl love you.'

'What should I do then?'

'Look into yourself, believe in yourself, make yourself better in each and every sphere of life. Speak the truth. Tell the person you love what is in your heart. Remember, you are not begging. Respect yourself first, only then you can respect the other person.'

"I listened carefully to what he said. He had changed my whole perspective. I told him that he had changed my whole thinking about the situation."

'Tell me one thing Robin Uncle, how do these so-called studs attract so many girls?'

'First thing – a stud is a temporary hero and not a legend. Just because he swaggers around using his parents' money doesn't mean anything. Getting large numbers of likes on networking sites does not mean anything. Listen, Ashish, if you want to become an admired person, then think about yourself. It is only when you do that, that you can help others. Make the mistakes – and learn from them. Then see how your life changes. Nothing will happen in one day, but definitely, they can be started in one day. You don't have to be great to start, but you have to start to be great.'

"I thanked him for his advice and went back to work.

"I started texting Kriti – asking about what she liked and what she liked to do in her free time and things like that. At that time, an hour seemed like a whole day waiting for responses to texts. When you see that the person has been active and not replied to you, you know how it is – it's like you've lost the war. You start thinking all kinds of things.

"Love is something that makes you do foolish things. But anything done for love is never silly to a person doing it! I wanted Kriti so much and I didn't care that she was older than I was. I just wanted her and that was that.

"I was going through a lot of problems then, mostly financial, and I needed emotional support. I knew what the reality was, but this mind of ours makes us do things that seem impossible at first, but work out in the end," said Ashish. He continued as I nodded.

"So when you believe in yourself, life becomes beautiful. Your tomorrows become mesmerising. Just walk with the attitude that I CAN, and you will get whatever you want. Just like the music in the background keeps going on, you go with the rhythm, get a reason to make your dreams bigger, make sure you write something new in the book of life every day. Have fun every day, live life awesomely, and when you find the road you are striving for, the smile will never go from your face and everything will be beautiful."

CHAPTER 3

ONE-SIDED LOVE

"Love is twisted. Only a few people know how to get it. It is a gift only a few have. There is passion in love. No one wants to lose a friendship while getting love, but sometimes it happens. One needs to take out time before committing to anything.

"It's not easy to give love in a relationship that gives you nothing in return. You want to do something so that the person remembers you. Always thinks of yourself and remember your good work.

"In one-sided love, people invest in a relationship, and that's what I did too. I persisted even when Kriti replied to me in monosyllables. There is nothing more powerful than unrequited love to break a heart. You suffer, and you suffer alone because suddenly this one person becomes the most important thing in your life. We perceive something sometimes, but the reality is totally different. That's why it is said don't give your heart to someone until you get one in return otherwise you will die. Love is not in our hands but going away from it is."

I had been listening to Ashish spellbound all this time. "So what did you do next?"

Just then, the air hostess came and asked what we would like to drink. Both of us asked for some wine and settled back into our seats. "Please finish," I begged, "because it will now be impossible for me to get off this plane without knowing the full story!"

Ashish smiled.

"I didn't quit or go away! How could I? It was impossible – being with someone as beautiful as Kriti, yet not with her. I fell more and more in love with her as I got to know her better. From her texts, it was obvious that she wasn't really interested in me, but I was hopeful that I would get her sooner or later – I was sure of that at least.

"The thing with beautiful women is that they are desired by many, but only a few who dare can get them. The one thing that kept me going was that she actually replied to my messages – even though they came very late.

"Actually I had never talked so much with any girl before. The only long conversation I recall was once with a girl called Karen – and that was 'hello, how are you?' to which her reply was 'Who are you?' I told her about myself and that I was a chef in a restaurant, but that was the end. She never replied after that! I was hurt for a while, but let it go because I didn't really know her and she didn't know me either.

"With Kriti, I knew it was for real. However, although I knew that my chances were very low and that I was taking a gamble, I was depending on my luck. I had a belief in myself this time. I was being optimistic – with the thought that if I try I will be able to do it.

"And so, even though I was a very impatient person, I calmed myself down and forced myself to be an optimist. I wanted Kriti in my life badly and I was willing to go to any lengths to get her. From our conversations, I discovered that she was a huge fan of Ranbir Kapoor! (Mainly through the heart emojis she added whenever she wrote his name) I shamelessly asked her if she would consider any other person other than Ranbir.

"To my surprise, she just replied with a 'hmm….' Anyhow, I handled the situation and asked if there were any other actors she was fond of. 'Yea, many…'

"I took a deep breath thinking of what to say next. The thing is that she was rich and famous and of course, very attractive – and that was probably why and how she had so many friends.

"And so it went on and on until one day I finally mustered up the guts to ask if we could meet. There was no reply from her for two whole days. I cursed myself for having asked her. At least she would have still been talking with me if I had not. I was distraught.

"I decided to put myself out of my misery. I texted her saying that if she didn't want to meet me, she should just come out with it and say no instead of ignoring me.

"My heart leapt when I heard the ping of the message on my phone. 'Hey, no! I'm sorry! I missed your message earlier and when you pinged me just now I saw it. Of course, I would love to meet you! When are you free? Is the weekend okay for you?'

"I was overjoyed. Although weekends were very busy for me at the restaurant, I had no other choice. I would take leave from work and meet her. 'Yea, let's meet this weekend,' I replied. 'Let me know where it is convenient for you.'

"However, three weekends passed and there was no sign of our meeting. We kept chatting but there was no meeting. I was waiting for a green signal from her. Finally, on the fourth weekend, she messaged me saying that she was going out with some friends and that we could meet if I was free. Of course, I was thrilled. She asked me to meet her at the United Colours Bar and Restaurant.

"I didn't even know where United Colours Bar was! I looked it up on Google maps quickly. When I saw the reviews, I was very nervous. It was an expensive place. I had just about 1800 rupees left to last me the rest of the month. How could I afford to go there? I decided to ask my mentor, Robin Uncle what to do. That evening, I went to the park to meet him. When I explained my situation, he gave 500 rupees. He also gave me 2000 rupees more. When I thanked him, he said, 'This is not a donation… don't worry…it's an investment.' I didn't understand what he meant at that time.

"My restaurant manager gave me the time off easily because I had never ever asked for leave earlier. He said that it would be difficult to manage without me but he would do something."

"United Colours Bar was about 3 km away. I chose to walk instead of taking the bus. I could see it from a distance – it was huge. I could hear the music from inside and there were a lot of well-dressed people going in and out. At the gate stood a 6-feet-tall bouncer. He looked at me suspiciously since I obviously didn't look like a regular. I paid the cover charge of 2000 rupees and walked in as confidently as I could.

"In my mind was the thought – two thousand rupees took care of my whole month's food and I spent it just like that on one night – just to see Kriti. It was worth it, I reassured myself. I wandered around a bit looking for her. Then I saw her.

"She was on the dance floor in a black dress with her hair swinging around her as she danced. My heart started thumping madly. I didn't know what to do next…in my dreams I had already proposed to her, but the reality was different.

"She caught my eye and came right up to me waving. 'Hey, Ashish!' She gave me a hug. I almost fainted when she did that but somehow managed to keep my cool.

'Hello, Kriti! It's been a long time!' She grabbed my hand and pulled me on to the dance floor. I protested saying that I don't dance and that I had never danced except at weddings.

'No problem,' she said. 'Come on! No one's looking. Anyway, when a girl asks you for a dance, you never say no.'

"And so I found myself on the dance floor shaking a leg with gusto watching her beautiful moves and telling myself how lucky I was.

'How's life?' she asked.

'Okay,' I managed to stutter. 'Can I get you something – juice, Pepsi, Coke?'

'I wouldn't mind a drink,' she said, 'bring me some juice with some vodka in it'. When she saw my shocked expression, she said, 'Let me guess…you don't drink do you?'

"I hemmed and hawed a little and finally told her that I didn't drink.

'Wow! It is legal for you to drink but you still don't. That's a nice change,' she said. Another brownie point I thought to myself. I went and bought her a juice with vodka and got myself a cranberry juice. She took the glass from me and drank it all in one shot. I was shocked but didn't show it. In my mind, I said 'what the fuck!'

"We danced for a bit with all her friends. I finally left at 1 am only because I had an early morning task of making sweets before getting ready for my regular job. I had taken it up to earn an extra 2000 per month to meet my expenses. I had started experimenting a lot at home with new recipes and the ingredients were very expensive.

"Kriti came up to me to say bye promising to meet soon again. I wanted to tell her that I loved her but just couldn't get myself to. I decided to walk home to clear my head. I never imagined that Kriti drank alcohol so it was a surprise for me.

"When you are in love, you have some expectations, but when it is one-sided love the expectations are unrealistic. That's what happens in love.

"With the technology we have today, we all want instant responses and when you know that your message has been received and read and you still haven't got a reply, you start getting worried. A hundred thoughts go through your head – is she upset with me, what have I done, why hasn't she replied? However, there's no point in getting worried because it usually turns out to be nothing more than a missed message. But until you do foolish things, how can it be love? Love has no age, anyone can fall in love with anyone at any time. There is something like love at first sight, but mostly it's infatuation. Most love stories start with infatuation but end with eternal love.

"Have you ever done whatever you have thought of doing? Be honest. Then how come you expect someone else to do it, always be correct? In love there is madness and this is needed when there is a huge difference between two people. Think before investing your emotions in a relationship...what you have been thinking about for so many days and finally, when you are just about to tell her what's in your heart, she introduces you to her boyfriend!

"That's the worst case scenario. People who are not good at making girlfriends or boyfriends mostly stay loyal when they get into a relationship. It's very important to give some time to understand each other. A person can be the most important person for you, but never let him or her be the only one. I always remember these lines. I had read them somewhere a long time ago and they had a powerful impact on me. I'm sure they will also have an impact on you if you change your way of looking at life."

Laugh like you're 10
Party like you're 20
Travel like you're 30
Think like you're 40
Advise like you're 50
Care like you're 60
Love like you're 70

CHAPTER 4

THE WORKOUT

"**I** became very conscious of my looks and body now. My mind was set on joining a gym to get a good physique. I wanted to lose weight desperately. I got Sadique to join the gym with me. The gym was on the 1st floor of a big building complex. I was getting a little tense about how much money I would have to shell out as fees. We met the gym instructor Karan, a tall guy with bulging biceps and baritone.

"He asked me what my weight was and said that he could transform me if I lost a little weight. I said I would try my best. Although I was talking to him, my mind was racing thinking about how much all this would cost. I almost choked when I was told that the monthly fee was 3000 rupees.

"Sadique noticed my crestfallen face and requested Karan to lower the fees a little as an exception. Karan took a deep breath, 'Look, friends, I can give you time till the end of month when I have to submit all my *hisaab*, but I'm sorry, rules are rules.'

"I then fixed the time for my workouts – I had to adjust to my part-time job and my regular job. I was lucky that the gym opened early, i.e., 5 am! I was always among the first few, if not the first to enter the gym every day thereafter. My routine now became more rigid – making me work harder, both mentally and physically.

"When I reached the gym at 5 am, there were four other people there already. Of these, Karan, the instructor was one of the; a married couple maybe in their 40s and one other person who would fit the perfect definition of a Mr Perfect.

"I went in and wished Karan who promptly put me on the treadmill next to Mr Perfect. I introduced myself to Mr Perfect. His name was Richard, and he was half Polish and half Indian, but 'fully Indian in culture'. He told me that he worked at an American bank as vice president of India's operations. I was surprised because he looked very young. He told me that he *was* young – he was only 27!

"We started talking and got to know each other better every day. And then one day, I told him about Kriti. I asked him if he had a girlfriend or a wife. He showed me his girlfriend's photo – she was beautiful, but not as beautiful as my Kriti. I told him that I needed help with how to go ahead with Kriti and asked if he would help me."

'Ashish, you're an honest lover so I will help you, but promise that you will not forget me.'

"I promised."

'I'm helping you because I see you as a successful person and I want to help you.'

"When I asked him how he knew that, he responded that he could see it through my passion, love and desire for cooking. 'You love what you do.'

"I was thrilled. **He said that the God above us has given the most difficult role of being the best actor.** He assured me that he would help me to reach the goal. In my excitement, I said okay not realising that he meant that the training would start immediately! He took me to the treadmill and set the speed to 10 and said run.

'You must be joking,' I said.

"But he wasn't! He told me to run, to run, run, run for Kriti, and most importantly, run for yourself. That was the day my training started for real. Day after day I started running for 20 minutes straight increasing the speed and then 20 minutes again in the evening at the park. Richard had motivated me so much that I was now determined to do everything to become perfect...so my training was in full form.

"I was doing 200 pushups, 200 crunches, 15-16 stretches, 30-40 pull-ups every single day. At first, it was really very difficult, but I was determined. Whenever I thought of giving up, Richard would remind me of Kriti and I would restart!

"Going to the gym became a habit and I was feeling better too. The once short fat kid started getting tight abs and my muscles started building up. I was getting popular at the gym too. It was a good feeling. I took the local train to the gym at 4.50 in the morning so that I would have enough time to work out and reach my workplace. I also dropped into a temple and church on my way to work every morning. It was a good routine and I was following it well. If for any reason I had to skip my workout or visiting the temple or church, I would feel lousy. I made sure that I kept up my routine and that made me feel energetic and enthusiastic about life.

"Kriti and I were talking, but our relationship didn't seem to be going anywhere. I felt that she was irritated with me asking so many questions. She never asked me anything so I kept feeling that she wasn't really interested in me. But I persisted."

"After 3 weeks Richard told me that he had paid my gym fees. I was happy but also surprised and asked why he did so. He said that when he was in trouble, nobody helped him so he knew the feeling. He said that he was in a position to help and wanted to do so, and that I shouldn't worry about it at all. I was very touched.

"And so another month passed. I was in extremely good shape. I kept going – and in case you're wondering how I got so badass at working out, there was one more reason.

"Well, the day I met Kriti at the bar, she had introduced me to her friends too. One of those girls was her classmate Parul, and my nightmare and problem, Pranay.

"It is quite ridiculous **when a girl says a boy is not her boyfriend but her best friend.** Pranay was a tall and good looking guy. He was a college president, a total stud and a fucking web developer and rich. Compared with him – I was nothing! This explained my determination in the gym. I mean, she had said 'not a boyfriend, but best friend'. It was confusing and infuriating at the same time.

"Richard listened to my rant and asked me softly, 'Ashish, do you love her?'

'Yes, I do'.

'Then the problem is solved,' he said.

"I didn't understand what Richard meant. He explained, 'If you want to become her hero then give her a reason to want to get close to you. Make her realise your importance.'

"The problem was that Pranay was taking advantage of Kriti by physically touching her. When I saw that, I wanted to kill him, but I controlled myself. When I told Richard, his reply was awesome. It struck a chord in my heart.

"He said that **if dogs run after a car, it doesn't mean that they can become the driver.** Believe in yourself because you love Kriti – you don't just want her physically, but also emotionally.

"I asked Kriti to meet me making an excuse that I needed some design-related help for a restaurant. She agreed and said she would meet me at the park. I was well on time – 5:30 pm and wandered around the park looking for her. She wasn't there so I waited on a bench for a few minutes.

"She looked exactly the same. Her lips were a faint pink colour and her hair was open. I saw her and started waving out to her and she waved back in response. I was just going to say something aloud in excitement, but I controlled myself.

"I really wanted to hug her, hold her for as long as possible, but I stopped myself and walked up to her calmly and shook hands. I could feel every single pair of eyes on us. I mean, me an ordinary guy with such a beautiful girl. I started talking to her – about any and everything else except the 'work' I had actually made an excuse about just to meet her!

"I stopped when she asked me about the work! I hemmed and hawed a little saying that the job was cancelled due to various reasons and that things hadn't worked out. I tried to justify my asking her to meet up.

'Ok, ok, no problem,' she said, 'I need to get back – I have projects to work on, so see you and catch you later.'

'Yea sure, can we please go for dinner or something?' I asked.

She smiled, 'Mr Ashish, are you asking me on a date?'

"I blushed, and said, 'No, no not at all, just dinner.'

'You cook, right?'

'Yes, I do!'

'Okay then, your home tomorrow!'

"I couldn't contain my excitement. She had actually agreed! But at that very moment, I suddenly realised that I couldn't call her over to my place – how could I? It was not a place she would be comfortable in. I quickly improvised.

'I'd love to have you over but my place is getting painted and it's in a mess.'

'Okay then, my place okay?'

"I felt as if someone had thrown a bucket of ice down my back. I couldn't believe my luck."

'Great idea Kriti! I will be there.' She bade me goodbye and left, 'Be there at 7 tomorrow.'

"I saw Robin uncle waving to me and I went to speak with him. He smiled when he saw me looking so happy. He congratulated me about my weight loss and was even happier to hear that I was to go over to Kriti's the next day."

CHAPTER 5

LOVE IS GREAT

"The next day at the gym I told Richard that I was going to meet Kriti that evening and that I was going to cook for her at *her* house, he congratulated me. 'Great job Ashish just keep going!'

"He told me to take my time over making a proposal and not to rush into it. 'Be slow and steady,' he said. 'You don't want to lose the friendship you have now, right? So take your time and tell her only when the time is right. And when you do, don't hesitate just speak it out loud. I nodded and went off to work.' Richard asked me to meet him before going in the evening refusing to tell me why.

"I wore my best clothes and dropped by to see Richard on the way to Kriti's house. He thrust a brown paper bag into my hands – to my surprise, it was a bottle of wine and a bottle of vodka!

"When I asked him why he said it was dating ritual. But when I told him that I didn't drink, he was surprised. I told him that I couldn't afford it. But it was good because Kriti did drink. 'So tell her you bought it for her – it will create a good impression on her.'

"Kriti lived alone. Although her family lived in the same city, she had moved out due to her busy work schedule. I rang the doorbell. I was mesmerised when she opened the door in a light blue dress up to her ankles. She had on my favourite light pink lipstick and was smiling. I was in my black blazer, blue jeans and white shirt.

"She was looking gorgeous and I kept staring at her. I finally found my voice when she shook me – 'Ashish, you've got something for me...'

"I handed her the bottles and entered the house looking around. She took me to the kitchen.

'So Mr Chef, show me what you can do!'

"I got to work immediately. She had already got all the ingredients I had asked for. I made all my signature dishes – gazpacho soup – a spicy cold tomato soup, halloumi and herb cakes for the main course, and tiramisu for dessert.

"I plated the food and poured the wine for her and we sat down for our meal. I was happy to show her that I was good at something.

"I told her, 'If I could give you one thing in life, I would give you the ability to see yourself through my eyes. Only then would you realise how important you are to me.'

"She smiled and started to pour the wine. When I said that I wouldn't have any, she held my hand and said to please try it once – 'for me'. How could I refuse when she spoke to me like that and looking straight into my eyes? I said I would try it, just for her. She poured the wine into the glass and got up to put on the music.

'I wish I could explain the feelings that I have for you, but that would take my whole lifetime,' I said to her. She just smiled.

"We ate all our food looking at each other. I didn't notice that she had finished her wine. I started blushing when I saw her looking at me romantically. She led me to her bedroom balcony from where we could see the lights of Mumbai across the sea. It was beautiful. I turned to look at Kriti and she happened to look at me at the same time. Our eyes made contact and soon we were just looking into one another's eyes.

"She lifted her hand and touched my right eyebrow and soon it moved down to my chin. I started getting a little uncomfortable so I said that I should leave.

'Wait, the flavour of the wine is just sinking in.'

"I panicked and insisted that I left. It was not that I didn't want to get physical, but I didn't want her to think that I was taking advantage of her in that condition.

'I need to go – it's almost midnight.'

'Don't you wanna finish this bottle of vodka?' she asked me teasingly.

'Good idea!' I took the bottle and said bye.

'What the hell Ashish?'

'You've drunk a lot and you need to sleep.'

"I had actually emptied my glass of wine into her glass when she went to put on the music and said that I had poured it from the bottle. So I knew how much she had drunk and how much I had had!"

'Okay, if you wanna go, go. It's your choice.'

"She pushed me out of the door saying good night and slammed the door hard on my face.

"I stood there for a while wondering what to do and then started walking down the stairs. Then something just happened and I suddenly did an about turn and ran up the stairs to her apartment on the 7th floor. I rang the doorbell urgently twice and then again. She opened the door after about 5 minutes and looked at me quizzically.

"I took a deep breath and said that I wasn't being able to get a cab. Then I said something that surprised even me. I said, 'Actually, I'm having a problem finishing this bottle and need someone to help me! Will you?'

"She suddenly grabbed me by the collar and pulled me towards her and started kissing me. I was shocked but also enjoyed the moment. I realised what was happening and pushed her back. She said very seriously that she was just trying to reduce my alcoholic state and started kissing me again.

"I kissed her back for a few seconds at the door and then lifted her up and took her into her bedroom. I placed her on the bed gently and opened the bottle of vodka and drank from it. Our clothes slowly slid off and we were soon in each other's arms.

"My eyes opened at 5 am like always. I looked around at the unfamiliar surroundings and was wondering where

I was. I looked down to see that I was not wearing a shirt and suddenly realised where I was! Kriti was fast asleep beside me. I smiled at the memory and got out of bed after planting a kiss on Kriti's forehead.

"I found my way to the kitchen and after opening all the cupboards found what I was looking for. I made some coffee for both of us and took it into the room. Kriti has just woken up and smiled at me lazily. My heart skipped a beat – she was looking even more beautiful than the night before.

'What's the plan for today?' she asked yawning and stretching.

'I'd love to spend the day with you but I have an interview this morning – it's at a 5-star hotel and I just can't afford to skip it – I really want the job.'

"Kriti looked sad for a minute, but smiled and said, 'Hey, it's okay. I know it's important so go ahead, but you must call me after you get free.' I promised.

"It was a good start to my day after a very long time and I was hopeful that it would turn out well. I took a cab back home and quickly got ready for the interview. I took a short detour to the temple before making my way to the hotel. I wanted to take blessings for my interview and thank God for all the good things happening to me.

"The hotel was huge. The imposing building took my breath away and I started feeling a little nervous. I thought to myself that if I did get the job there, my life would change. I would be able to pursue my dreams. I had been writing all the recipes of all my signature recipes and was hoping to find a publisher for it. I had already been rejected by seven publishers because I was not what they would call a 'reputed' chef. They had not heard about me and were not willing to take a risk with an 'unknown'. So becoming a chef at a well-known 5-star hotel would definitely give wings to at least one of my dreams.

"I was a little nervous as I entered and went up to the reception to ask where the interviews were being conducted. A smart young woman led me to the main kitchen of the hotel. I looked around in awe. The kitchen was huge and had all the latest gadgets. It was just the place that I needed to make my signature dishes. I was now determined to get the job.

"There were about 30 people for the interview. We were given a test – to cook our best dish in 1 hour. The head chef met us and put us at ease as he recounted his tough journey to becoming one of the top chefs in the country. He then gave us instructions for the test, 'You have the liberty to pick up anything from our store and create your best dish.' The shocker was that only one person would be selected from the 30 there!

"And so the test started. I decided to make a dessert because desserts are my speciality. However, while taking the ingredients, I panicked and missed out on the main flavouring agent. You know how it is when it comes to perfection – half a spoon extra of salt or sugar can make all the difference. Of course, it was obvious that nobody would lend it to me – seeing the cut-throat competition. I was about to make the flavour using another method naturally, but one of my co-competitors felt sorry for me and offered me the flavouring agent I was hunting for. I thanked him profusely and took it. But by the time I realised that he had handed me the wrong agent, it was too late!

"My dessert was a disaster! I was totally shaken up. The day that had started so beautifully was now crumbling right in front of me. I left the hotel and went straight back home. When Kriti texted me, I had nothing to say. For the first time, I was not happy or excited to receive a message from her. I was in total shock. How could I have messed up so badly? Why didn't I read what was given to me? I didn't feel like meeting anyone or going anywhere. I sat and brooded the whole day and finally, in the evening, I psyched myself to get out of it. I forced myself to forget what happened and to learn from it.

"My thoughts went back to the night before and I smiled. I had fallen head over heels in love. It was not just physically. I had finally found someone who would understand me.

"However, my thoughts kept going back to the chance I had missed and as much as I tried to erase that bad memory, I was not being able to. I kept asking God why everything cannot be good at once and why when one good thing happens, a bad one happens too – was God trying to maintain an equilibrium or what?

"I shifted my focus and worked even harder to make it better. I started working relentlessly – I knew that that was the only cure. I loved my work – more than anything else, I would even leave Kriti for it! And that was something!

"When in love, you know things start happening… you start feeling everything differently, you forget things, you start singing and smiling even when you are alone. Everything looks nice and happy – you start meeting people more warmly, everything starts looking more colourful and beautiful, you start taking care of yourself and become slightly obsessed with how are you looking, you never miss a chance to look into the mirror...

"Kriti and I met every evening at the park. I would see Robin Uncle at a distance and smile and wave at him. I wanted to introduce Kriti to him but something or the other always came in the way.

"I dropped into Kriti's place one day and to my surprise, she was smoking! She had never smoked in front of me earlier and I didn't smoke myself so it was a shocker. I didn't want to tell her that I had never smoked so I just said that I was not in the mood. When I asked her when she started smoking, she looked quite offended."

'Look, Ashish, I'm in the fourth year and 3 years older than you. You know that all this happens in college – it's liberating. Everybody does it and so I started too. No big deal.' I just nodded. She asked if I smoked and I said that I did. She didn't seem to believe me and dared me to smoke one with her. Of course, I couldn't – started coughing and spluttering. She started laughing. 'This is a herbal cigarette! I was just having fun with you and you really did get fooled!'

"She cupped my face with her two hands gently, 'I don't smoke Ashish. I just wanted to see your reaction.'

"She hugged me and gave me a peck on my cheek. Then she told me that she was going to Singapore for an exhibition for about a week. 'So I was thinking – let's do something fun today.' We were just about to get romantic when I got a call about a medical emergency that I had to rush out for."

CHAPTER 6

THE BREAK-UP

"I met Kriti the night before she left for Singapore. My head was on her lap and her hand was playing with my hair after a steamy lovemaking session. I blurted out that I loved her. I was thrilled when she replied that she loved me too!

"But something was amiss. I got up and held her hands and said 'I love you'."

'Ashish, you're not serious na?'

'Of course I am Kriti.'

"She was quiet for a while. Then she said, Ashish listen, I don't know what to say – there's been a misunderstanding.'

'What misunderstanding? That's the most ridiculous thing I have ever heard! A misunderstanding? About what? What about our meetings, dates…and our relationship?'

'You are a good person but I am not in love with you. I just went along with you – you were sweet and caring and always there for me. I'm sorry – I know this is not easy – but I was just going along, not thinking of anything.'

"I didn't know how to react, what to say. I just stood there in silence. Finally, I managed to say something. 'Why? Why did you just lead me on? Why are we together? What about everything we did together?'

'Hey! Why're you getting so serious? I never thought that you loved me – I thought that all you guys are alike and that we were using each other for physical benefits only.'

"I was shocked. I couldn't speak and just stared at Kriti. I held her shoulders and asked, 'You're joking, right?'

"She took my hands and pushed me back and said, 'Listen, face it! You know you've been lucky to get someone as hot as me to sleep with me – but now, it's over. Get over it! I don't love you!'

"I tried to reason with her but she was in no mood to listen."

'I don't want to talk to you Ashish, please just go away now.'

"I refused to leave like that. I had become very emotional by then and kept rambling. 'You've not given me a proper answer – I will not leave! I will not!'

"She was livid and literally pushed me against the wall."

'Okay, so you want to know the problem? Let me tell you! I really didn't want to but since you're insisting, here it is…look, Mr Ashish, what you earn in a whole month is what I spend on myself at the beauty parlour in one day…second, my father is the owner of a big chain of hotels in which you can't even think of getting a job… third, you're way shorter than me…fourth, I'm older than you and also more intelligent. And after all that's happened today, to me you're just a below-average guy trying hard to make something of your life. I don't know if I can wait for so long – I see myself as a successful designer in the next 2-3 years. What about you? You'll still be struggling to get a foothold in your industry. Now, do you see? Do you still think that I will hold your hand and get married to you? If you are, then you're only fooling yourself.'

"I stood there shell-shocked at her words. Before I could say anything more, she continued, 'Look, Ashish, you are a good person but nothing more than that. In today's world, you may be a good person but if you have nothing else, then you're doomed. You may not be a good person but have money and fame – that'll get you far!'

"I controlled my tears took a deep breath."

'I thought we shared a good bond – both physically and emotionally. We did share everything equally but the reality is that there were actually never two people in this relationship – there was only one – me. I was the fool who invested my time and emotions and dreamt of having a life with you,' I said, looking down at my feet.

'Sorry. I made a mistake. I thought you were a normal guy but you turned out to be something else. Some things are just not possible in our life and this is one of them. So stop chasing them and look for something else. Ashish, I am requesting you to leave. I don't want to meet you again. Let's not make this unpleasant.'

"I felt like slapping her at that moment but controlled myself."

'Okay Kriti, I'm leaving. Thank you for teaching me such an important thing about myself – I am nothing. Nothing in front of you. Goodbye Kriti and good luck!'

"I left her apartment in a huff. I just couldn't get over what she had said about being just another guy who was only thinking of physical needs. Did she mean what she said? I know I was nothing compared to her and she was older than me too but then why did he give me hope? I was devastated. I walked on thinking about what had happened not knowing where I was going. I found myself in front of a cheap bar near my house. My feet automatically took me inside.

"I smiled to myself. Life had proved me wrong once again. I needed to celebrate. I don't know whether I was being foolish or optimistic at that time. For the very first time, I walked into a bar myself for myself. It was a bar that served local liquor, with dim lights and c-grade songs playing. Almost everyone inside looked like a criminal to me. It was a terrible place but I was in somewhat the same condition – completely broken. I walked in and sat at an empty table.

"When the waiter asked me what I wanted, I told him to bring me whatever he could to stop my blood tears. He stared at me for a while and then got me something to drink. It tasted awful but I glugged it down and told him to get me another. Then I got another and another. I don't know how long I sat there doing this. I didn't realise what I was doing till two people came up to me."

'What's the matter? This is your 8th drink – you will fucking die. Stop it!'

'Either this way or that, I'm dead already,' I slurred, 'and even if I stay alive I will die sooner or later. I am not happy – that bitch left me…sorry, sorry, I am sorry for my tone… that respected bitch left me!'

"As they stared at me, I continued, 'She told me that there was nothing between us, without even thinking for a second what this relationship means to me. You know, one-sided love is a cancer if you don't get it first and get late in identifying it. You will die in the ugliest manner you can imagine. This whole process is a bloody therapy which leads to your own disaster.'

"They listened for a while and convinced me to leave to avoid getting into further trouble. They led me out of the bar and I managed to show them where I lived. They dropped me there and I somehow managed to walk up to my room on the first floor. I took out the key to open the front door but before I could do so, I passed out.

"When my eyes opened, it was morning and I found a bunch of people looking down at me as I lay on the ground in front of my room. I jumped up and quickly let myself into my room. After a quick cup of coffee, I showered and left for work.

"I tried my best to concentrate on my work but all I could see was Kriti's face in front of me. I just couldn't focus on my work. All I wanted to do was to call Kriti and hear her say it was a big mistake and that she didn't mean any of what she had said to me. But I didn't. Who was wrong here and who was right? I loved her but her arguments made sense – I was actually nothing.

"That evening, I went to meet Robin Uncle at the park. He was very happy to see me after so long. After a little chit-chat about everyday things, I narrated the whole incident to him.

'I appreciate your love young man. Even after she has said so much to you, you still love her. But Ashish, listen, in any kind of love relationship, the person should be important to you, but not so important that you forget about everything else, your dreams, your ambitions, yourself.'

"I nodded, getting emotional. He patted my back and said, 'You are a very mature person and better off than many others of your age. You loved someone not for any kind of benefit but by heart for love. It was and will remain pure. Have faith.'

"I told him how I was just jot able to concentrate on anything however much I tried. I wanted to get over it but was just not able to. He replied, 'This is love my friend, it will take time.'

'Love is very complex, but now I have to change my priorities, I have to pursue my dreams.'

"I was clear that I had to do something in life and I really wanted to be successful and would go to any lengths to achieve it. However, my routine had changed – I was sleeping less and less and spending more and more time at bars drinking and smoking. I knew it was wrong but it was a relief for me so I went on doing it. I followed Kriti through her updates on Facebook and Instagram – I always knew what she was doing, where she was and what was going on in her life. Many times, I would dial her number only to disconnect it immediately.

"I kept re-living the way she pushed me against the wall. I had wanted to say so many things at that time but couldn't say them. One always hears of people becoming poets, singers or like my case, writers when they are sad. And how right they are.

"My eyes search for you and my mind wonders how I live without you, without you how I live. How many promises you made and in one go, broke...all I know is that you have not left me forever, but just for a while. Please come back – I want to kiss you when my lips are dry, I want to hold you when I'm about to cry.

"All I could think of was how to get her back in my life. While walking by the gym, I bumped into Richard and told him about what had happened. He found it hard to believe and tried to comfort me as much as he could. I felt I had become a rotten autumn leaf – it was as if someone had frozen my heart and broken it in one go.

"Kriti's status update on Facebook mentioned someone she seemed to be sharing a special relationship with. 'Our relationship cannot be described in words...I was like, what the hell...I spent so much time with her and here she is writing this for someone else. *And* she is actually with someone else! I felt lousy. Why had I wasted so much time on her? I regretted it so much. She didn't realise that the person who loved her truly was me. Then, when I saw a picture of the person she was referring to in her post, I was even more devastated. He was good looking and smart and seemed to be doing very well in life. I looked at myself in the mirror. I now had a beard and my regular smoking and drinking had made my face look leathery and lifeless. I turned away immediately – I couldn't bear to look at myself.

"A week later, Richard called and wanted to meet that evening. As soon as he saw me he gave me a tight hug and said that he had been thinking of me and the rough patch I was going through. 'So I thought I'd get you over to chill out a bit. We're going to partaaaaay!!!' he was in a really fun mood. His mood was infectious and I started actually looking forward to partying the night away.

"We went to one of the really happening bars and ordered some drinks for ourselves. There was a special DJ that evening and the music was awesome. I started getting pumped up and when he pushed me towards the dance floor, I lost all my inhibitions and started dancing madly. I was so immersed in my dancing that I forgot about all my problems. Jumping and dancing and fucking rocking... singing like mad. The madness carried on – drink after drink and song after song. Richard had organised for a driver to drop us home so there was no problem. 'Just have fun...Ashish...don't worry about a thing. Whatever happens, happens for a reason, usually a good reason so no worries bro! Life has a way of sorting things out... enjoyyyyyy!'

"When I took a break to use the bathroom, Richard came up to me asking if I had a picture of Kriti. When I took it out, he handed me his lighter and asked me to burn it. 'It'll make you feel even better,' he said. I hesitated a bit and slowly lit the lighter and touched it to the edge of the photograph...and what do you know? I felt so relieved. I was feeling better already!

"I don't fucking care anymore – it's over. Let her go to hell. I don't give a damn anymore. She thinks that she can make me feel bad forever – well, she's wrong!" I was screaming in the bathroom not noticing anyone else around me. I was free at last."

'So now Ashish, now that you're free from Kriti, make yourself more presentable. And you'll have all the girls falling for you. Update your pictures on Facebook and Insta and of course, Tinder, and spread the word. You're ready to party once again.'

"We went back to dance floor and partied some more. Everything seemed so much better – especially when you decided that you didn't care anymore. I noticed some girls sitting at the bar and checking me out. I was feeling better already! We left the bar arm in arm singing at the top of our voices. I thanked Richard for showing me such a wonderful night as I got off the car. I just about managed to get into my room and fell off to sleep as soon as my head hit my pillow."

CHAPTER 7

MIRACLES DO HAPPEN

"And so life went on. I was feeling better but my routine was pretty much the same – drinking, smoking and partying hard. Even though I had put Kriti out of mind, she was still lurking around somewhere in my heart. Every time I picked up a drink or a cigarette, I would feel her around me. Strange but true.

"One day, I was at the restaurant following orders when we were told that the renowned chef was coming to our restaurant for his show Indian Food Rocks. When we were told that it was Gordon Ramsay, there was huge excitement all around – but also a lot of nervousness because he was known to be a scathing critic. However, to me, it was like my gateway to happiness. If I could impress him with my food then my life would change forever. I had two hours to prepare. I decided on my dish and gathered all the ingredients. I had to make it. Gordon Ramsay was my idol and if he was coming I couldn't afford to make a single mistake.

"The crew arrived and set up the place. A little while later, Gordon Ramsay walked in. All of us clapped as he came in and he smiled back and said thank you. My manager knew that he was my idol and gave me full freedom to handle the kitchen as my own that day. I was thrilled. I went up to Gordon to take his order. I was shivering in excitement and although he saw it, he pretended that he had not noticed. 'Bring me the best of what you have.' I nodded and came back. My crew and I had made all the preparations and I went in to prepare the plate. The director of the show came in to check the plating so that it looked good on camera too and gave us the go-ahead.

"I walked out with the plate and placed it in front of him gently on the table. He nodded and smiled as I walked back in. As he picked up his fork, I took a deep breath and said a little prayer in my mind. He put the first morsel of food into his mouth and stopped for a second...then started chewing again. He paused for another second and took a sip of the water in front of him. Then he stood up abruptly and walked up to me. I was shivering. Before he could say anything, I said, 'Sorry sir.'

"He looked a little puzzled, then smiled and patted me on my shoulder. 'This is one of the best preparations of Indian food that I have ever tasted!'

"I thought I heard wrong. But when I heard the huge applause, I realised what he had said and started smiling. It was like getting the president's award!

"The next thing I heard Gordon saying was that he wanted to work with me! I was ecstatic. This was something I had been dreaming of for years and years. And now my dream was finally coming true. He called me over to his hotel that evening to discuss some things.

"I met Robin Uncle at the park that evening to tell him about this. He congratulated me and gave me his blessings. 'See, I told you that you would get whatever you want – if you kept going. And see you have got one of the things you really wanted…watch now, you will get everything else as well.'

"I rushed home to get dressed for the meeting with Gordon. I wore my best clothes and shoes and slathered on some cologne. I got reminded of my first date with Kriti. And then I happened to check my phone and saw that she had recently updated her picture with some other guy. I felt a twinge of sadness but quickly put it out of the way – I didn't want to jeopardise my meeting with Gordon in any way.

"I realised that I was going to the same hotel to meet Gordon that I had messed up in. What irony! I laughed at myself, paid the cab and confidently walked into the foyer and up to the reception. I was shown up to the Presidential Suite. Gordon was waiting for me along with the head chef of the hotel (I recognised him from his uniform). Gordon welcomed me warmly and introduced me to the chef. He looked like he remembered me from somewhere but couldn't place me – I was much relieved.

'Listen Ashish, I want you to join Chef Sam here as an assistant chef. I don't know how much you're already getting paid, but we can offer you…(it was almost 4 times the salary I was drawing!).'

"I took a deep breath – it was all going very very fast. Then he said, 'And that's not all – if you do well here, I want to take you to London as head chef of our new restaurant there!'

"My words died in my throat. I couldn't speak – as I looked up at Gordon, a tear rolled down my cheek. I quickly wiped it away and told them that I accepted the offer. He proffered his hand and I took it. He picked up an envelope from the table and handed it to me. It was an advance joining cheque of two lakh rupees! I walked out of the hotel that evening with my head held high. I was now the second in command of the kitchen of the hotel that I had exited from in disgrace just a few months ago!

"I hailed a cab and headed straight to the expensive bar I had first met Kriti in. Money really boosts your morale and confidence. Now I could go anywhere in a cab, walk into any restaurant, go shopping, and buy myself whatever I wanted. I walked into the bar with my head held high and ordered the most expensive drink there was in the menu.

"How things change! Just one day ago I was broke and depressed. I didn't know what I would do, where I would go and what would happen and here I was today, about to start a great new job with a lot of money in my bank and looking at a great future. The journey to my success had started, but there was a long way to go.

"I suddenly got reminded of the bar I had gone to on the break-up night. It reminded me of the situation I was in at that time, but somehow it was more comforting to me than this staid, silent bar with soft music playing and pretentious people all around speaking in hushed tones.

"So after one drink, I went back to that bar. It was just as I remembered it to be. I ordered a few drinks and sat there for a bit – to remind myself of the condition that I was in then.

"I started work at the hotel and every day it was a new experience. I worked hard and learnt new things. I knew I was becoming better and better. I realised that the only cure to my sadness was my work so I kept working and working as much as I could.

"It had been two months since I started working there. I now had a long beard and dressed sharply. People started to recognise me and there were reviews of my new recipes everywhere. I was getting job offers from other big hotels too. I couldn't think of leaving that hotel – I knew I had a lot more to learn and I wanted to be the best in my field. I promised myself that I would look for better opportunities only when I felt that I had had my fill there and had no more to learn.

"Success is not the absence of failure – it is something that happens when preparation meets opportunity. I was getting better every day. I was working hard and I was happy. I added to my book of recipes every night. Most nights, I would still be reminded of Kriti and my hands would itch to call her, but I would control myself. This continued for weeks.

"Finally, three months got over and I got the approval for the London restaurant. I was really excited as it was the first time I would be flying! And that too, internationally. I went shopping for new clothes and shoes with my friends. I had money to buy the things I needed without having to minge on anything. Everything was on track now – except my broken heart. But I was more mature now – time had taught me to be silent, to live with the pain, to accept sorrow.

"No doubt my financial position was getting better, and my emotional condition was better but I just couldn't stop thinking of her. I mean she was the only girl I had ever dated so I suppose it was understandable.

"I was nervous about travelling alone to London and requested Richard, my gym pal to come along with me. I had never been on a plane and the thought of flying 8 hours straight was very daunting to me. Luckily he had some official work and was flying out to another city on the very same day. I was thrilled to have someone with me at least till the airport.

"On the way to the airport, he coached me on what to say and how to go about checking in and immigration and I was grateful for the tips. He left me at the international departure and I waved him goodbye. The girl at the ticket counter was very smart and polite. She asked if it was my first international flight and when I said yes, she handed me a form to fill in. She then helped me to fill it in and guided me about how to go through after checking in. I could hear numerous announcements one after the other. I saw some people eating hurriedly and some standing at counters for their turn to get coffee, tea or some other beverage. I was feeling like having some coffee but seeing the line, I decided not to and sat down near the gate to hear my flight announcement.

"I was lucky to discover a middle-aged man sitting beside me going on the same flight. When I told him how nervous I was to be travelling for the first time, he said not to worry. 'Go get something to eat or drink – you'll feel better.'

"I bought myself a sandwich and went back and sat down. As soon as the flight was announced we walked towards the gate to enter the aircraft. I got a window seat. A very distinguished, oldish and very well-dressed man in a kurta-pyjama sat beside me. I smiled at him as the announcement for fastening seatbelts came on. I was terrified when the plane started hurtling down the runway and took deep breaths.

"I fell off to sleep almost immediately. The anxiety and tension had got me very tired. I chit-chatted with my neighbour over our meal. When we reached, he was very gracious and said not to worry about anything in London. 'If you get into a problem, just yell out some abuses in Hindi and there will a number of Indians ready to help you out! This is your first trip and a first trip comes only once so enjoy it to your fullest.'

"I took a taxi to the address I was told to report at. After freshening up a bit, I went to the restaurant to see my place of work. The staff was very friendly and helpful and gave me small tips about how to get around in London.

"I reported to work the next day and got straight to work. There was a lot to be done. I had to work doubly hard – it was my job to make people love Indian food and make them keep coming back for more.

"It had been 6 months since I came to London. I had made many new friends and spent a lot of time looking around the city and at bars. I could, at last, say that I had made something of myself – I had enough money to spend, I had a good place to live in and I had a fantastic job that I loved.

"It had also been a long time since I last spoke with Kriti."

"I don't know what came over me one night when after a few drinks at my favourite bar, I dialled Kriti's number. Her cousin answered the call."

'Can I speak to Kriti please?'

'Just a moment…Kriti…there's a call for you.'

"My heart skipped a beat when I heard her voice."

'Hello…who's this?'

"I was silent for a few seconds not knowing what to say.

'Is this Ashish?' she asked softly.

'Ashish, head chef, The Great Hotel, London.'

'Congratulations! Great to hear from you after so long. By the way, my studies get over in a couple of months and I've got a placement in a *Fortune 500* company.'

'Good! You deserve it.'

'So Ashish, when you are coming back to India?'

'Why?'

'Well, I think we should meet sometime.'

'Kriti, all decisions you cannot take,this decision is mine not yours to make. you decided that you don't want see me again and now it's my choice that I want to see you or not. Bye, good to have connected after so long.'

"I ended the call and took a sip of my drink smiling. I thought that went quite well.

"Months passed and I got two weeks off to visit India. I was nervous because I was going back home after so long.

I bought gifts for everyone but was still wary of how they would greet me.

"I rang the bell and my father opened the door with a newspaper in his hand. He smiled and hugged me. 'Son, I am so happy to see you. How was the flight from London?'

"I thought I was giving them a surprise but I was surprised...I don't know how they knew that I now lived in London. My mother rushed out and hugged me and congratulated me.

"Apparently they were in touch with my friends who kept them updated about me – where I was, what I was doing, how I was doing. 'We kept tabs on you son, we wanted you to succeed on your own – and were there to help – but now are so proud that you never gave up and did everything on your own,' said my mother.

'Well done son, well done...I am proud of you... proud...very proud,' said my father. I was surprised to see his reaction and also very happy. He had finally realised that I could do things on my own.

"My two best friends dropped by a little later shouting and cheering with a cake to welcome me. We had so much to talk about. I told them about my life in London and showed them pictures. They told me that my old restaurant manager wanted to meet me about some book of that I had left behind. It was then that I remembered that I had left my book of recipes with him.

"I went to the restaurant the next day. I looked around nostalgically – recalling the day I joined, my first salary, the kitchen where I worked for hours on end."

'Welcome son,' said my old manager hugging me. 'A great chef in London now, huh? Congratulations! So proud of you son, you did great. I always knew that you would do something big in life.'

"I gave him the watch that I had got for him. He became very emotional and hugged me again. 'A boy who used to take a salary from me is today giving me a gift. Love you son…god, bless you.'

"When I asked about my book, he told me that my book was actually somewhere in America! I was shocked.

'Don't panic! Remember the crew that came with Gordon Ramsay to shoot the street series…? Well, after you left I found your book and read it. That book can make anyone fall in love with cooking.'

'Thanks but what about the America thing?'

'So after the shoot when most people had left, I called one person from the crew and asked him to give this book to the chef.'

"Apparently, the chef was bowled over and handed it over to this international publisher to publish it. The condition was that I had to keep it secret until we got the publisher.

"I was thrilled. First my family, and now this! I hugged the manager and thanked him. 'You have helped me so much – I will always remember your kindness till I die. Please call me whenever you need any help – I will be honoured to be of any kind of help to you.'

"All of a sudden, my life seemed to have become rosy. Everything was falling into place. However, when all this happens in reality, life gets boring. We need thrills, excitement and suspense in life. But what I had seen in my past was more than enough to teach me life's game and how it works. I partied hard with my friends, met many new people and was having the time of my life. I managed to buy a house in Mumbai with the savings I had made in London. Now in two days, I was flying back to London.

"One day before I left I went to meet Robin Uncle at the park. We sat on the same bench we always sat on. We talked about the change in my life and he asked me about life in London. We talked and laughed a lot. I hadn't realised how much I had missed talking to him. Then he asked me about Kriti, about whether I had heard from her. 'Yes, we talked once but you know things are very complicated and it's difficult to get back. I may meet her tomorrow.'

"I left after a while. 'God bless you son,' he said. As he walked me to the gate, he mentioned to me that he knew someone who was Kriti's relative and that he had told him that Kriti was leaving for America. She'd apparently got a job there.

'I didn't want to tell you but I just couldn't keep it away either. Listen now, the choice is yours...I don't know what you can do or want to do but it will be nice if you both can get back together. You're made for each other...you look good together – like a perfect photo,' he concluded.

"I didn't know how to react so I just said thanks and left. I took a cab and went back home stopping midway for a bottle of wine. Her favourite one. I don't know why I did that.

"Once home, I opened my laptop and started going through our old pics. I had opened the bottle of wine and was drinking directly from it. As usual, my hand went to my phone and dialled her number. I disconnected as soon as I had dialled. I put my phone aside and slept. I woke up with a start at 4 am. I dreamt that Kriti was getting married to someone and I was clapping and giving her a gift. I found myself sweating profusely.

"I drank some water and lay down again to try and sleep but sat up again – I would not marry Kriti but could not see her going away with someone else either. I dialled her number immediately and didn't hang up this time. But guess what – she didn't pick up the phone! Why does it always happen when you need something it gets more difficult to get it.

"My mind started racing. I was now fully awake. It was about 5:30 am. I knew that Robin Uncle would be awake and called him. Thank god he answered.

'What happened Ashish? Is everything alright?'

'No Uncle, nothing is okay. I didn't know that I wanted Kriti but now I know that I do. And I don't know what to do!'

'Congratulations! You have finally realised!'

'Wait, wait, Uncle, which flight is she taking? And when? Can you please find out for me?'

'Ashish, are you okay?'

'I was not – but now I am.'

'She's leaving on the Air India flight at 9 am.'

"I looked at the clock – it was 6:15 am. I dialled Sadique's number."

'What the hell man? It's 6 am! What do you want?'

'No time for questions Sadique, please meet me at the Central Avenue Centre immediately. Am calling Abhinav too.'

'But why?'

'I'm going to propose to Kriti.'

"I used some really colourful language to explain the situation and eventually got them out of bed. They reached within 15 minutes. I had asked them to get their passports and some money too since we were going to the international terminal. The airport was not very far luckily so I had hope. I told them that I would tell them the details on the way.

"I explained that Kriti was leaving for America forever and that this was my last chance of meeting her. And also that I had had a really bad dream. They listened to me but were unable to understand the urgency. We rushed into the airport."

'Stop…stop…are you running in a park or what?' the security guards stopped us from entering.

'Sir, please, we're in a real hurry…'

"I looked at my watch – it was 7:45. I had very little time. I couldn't afford to lose this chance."

'Why? What happened?' he asked.

'Death…very sick relative…accident,' all three of us blurted out at the same time.

"The guard stared at us questioningly. I quickly recovered and told him that a relative had met with an accident was on his deathbed, so we needed to reach there as fast as we could. We showed him our passports.

'Ok, ok go. Don't panic.'

"We entered the airport after thanking him profusely and looked for the Air India counters. They were all super crowded. I rushed in and said that I needed to board the flight to America now!"

'Sir, sir, please calm down. Let me see what I can do. Okay…there's a flight at 10 am but it's full.'

"I begged her – I told her that I had to be on it. Please understand that someone will die and that we'd be separated forever if I didn't get on the flight."

'I understand Sir, but it's simply not possible.'

"My friends looked at me sadly. 'Man, it's really not possible. You've lost this time…just accept it'.

"When you feel like everything is over and there is nothing left, believe me, everything is still possible. My friends had turned around to leave and I was about to follow them when at that very moment I saw the captain and crew of the Air India flight walking towards security. I pointed to them and told my friends – 'Look – that's how we're going on to the flight!'

'We just need to get into those uniforms!'

"We noticed that the pilot had stayed behind to get a cup of coffee. I told Abhinav and Sadique that we had to somehow make the coffee or something fall on his clothes. I begged them to do something. I was so desperate.

"Sadique and Abhinav walked into the cafe and carried out the scene like something right out of a James Bond film. Abhinav bumped into the waiter and the juice fell on the pilot."

'What the hell!' cursed the pilot standing up immediately looking down at his ruined shirt.

'Sorry Sir, really sorry,' said Abhinav.

"The pilot started yelling at Abhinav like a mad man. Sadique picked up the bunch of napkins and tried to clean him up.

"The pilot shooed them both off and rushed into the washroom. Our plan was working. All three of us followed him into the washroom. When he saw us he started cursing again. I walked up to him menacingly and said that we needed his uniform."

'Why? Why do you need my uniform? This is wrong. I cannot give it to you...' and then as an afterthought, he looked at us suspiciously, 'Are you terrorists?'

'Nope, not a terrorist, just a lover!'

"I kept requesting him humbly and politely but he refused. Abhinav picked up the fire extinguisher and whacked him on the head with it."

'What the fuck did you do Abhi?'

'Hey don't worry, I didn't hit him too hard! He's not dead. Do you want Kriti or not?? Now go..go…go!'

"I quickly changed into the pilot's uniform and walked towards the plane very confidently looking around all the while. I finally spotted Kriti sitting and reading a book. I smiled and walked straight up to her."

'Hi, Kriti!'

"She looked up at me surprised and stood up to go."

'Please sit. I have something to say to you…please listen to me. After that, you can leave if you want.'

"She stared at me in shock looking me up and down in the pilot's uniform."

'Forget everything and just look into my eyes, please Kriti.'

'Ashish…'

'Shhh…just do as I say please. Dear Kriti, I have been thinking about us a lot. How do I sum it up…I don't know. I know it's not been perfect but Kriti, when are together it's the most beautiful thing in the world…the hangovers… bottles of wine…the packets of cigarettes you've got me addicted to…and also to you. The gorgeous insanity. After you've gone, there's been no sunset or sunrise in my life. It may seem that there is nothing left between us, but believe me, if you close your eyes and listen to the whisper of your heart you will feel the love. I just wanted to say this to you. Thanks for listening.'

"There was complete silence for a few seconds and then after what seemed like an eternity, she stood up and hugged me."

'I love you Ashish. I'm sorry for all the things I said to you but maybe the conditions were not right at that time. I was wrong about you.' She hugged me yet again.

'Grandpa, he's the one I was talking about…'

"I turned to look at who she was talking to and to my utter surprise, it was Robin Uncle! I was shocked."

"I smiled and shook my finger at him…as if to say, so you knew all along…"

'You two know each other?'

'Yes…long story!' I said. 'If he hadn't told me that you were leaving, I would never have come this far. Thank you Uncle.'

'But I'm only going for 3 weeks!'

"I looked at Robin Uncle and he put up his hands smiling. 'Guilty as charged. But look at it like this – if I hadn't lied, you would probably not have come so far!' "

The seatbelt sign came on as the stewardess made the statutory announcements. I salute you Ashish! This was way better than any movie I have ever seen. What an awesome flight you made it for me. I will always remember it. I asked what the status was now with Kriti and him.

Ashish replied, "We got married a month later and now have 3 children! Today I'm a multi-millionaire thanks to the TV shows, restaurants and books."

"Rohit, always remember, if you think that something is impossible and you know someone who is doing it then let the person do it. Because it is the crazy ones who change the world."

I gave Ashish a huge hug at the luggage carousel. "All the best for your future."

He smiled and said, "It was really good recalling my story...and telling it to you. Thanks for listening!"

He gave me the address for the book launch and we exchanged numbers promising to keep in touch. While he lives happily ever after, I, the writer of this book is still searching for my Kriti.

EPILOGUE

Have the courage to follow your passions because that is the only way to make your dreams and desires come true.

And you have to keep trying and trying to get what you want. Don't get misled by others. Nobody can decide for you. Don't let anyone interfere in your dreams. Say aloud – I will make it and no matter how hard it gets, I will keep giving my best every single time.

Things to take from this book

1.   Believe in yourself

2.   Think success, never failure

3.   Trust. Keep your belief that one day you will earn what you deserve.

4.   Just keep working until expensive becomes cheap.

I hope you have liked this book. If you have, then ask others to read it too. Don't lend your copy to them, rather ask them to buy a copy for themselves. And yes, I am a little greedy because it's my first book! I want it to be a big success so please help me!

DARE TO LOVE,
LIVE. MAKE YOUR LIFE AWESOME.

ROHIT CHAWHAN

EPILOGUE BY ANURAG BATRA

Young is the New Wise

"For every child prodigy that you know about, at least 50 potential ones have burned out before you have even heard about them."

Itzhak Perlman

I am sure Rohit Chawhan is not one of the above. Rohit is a child prodigy in the making and reading his maiden book will give you that experience and confidence.

I believe synchronicity is God s way of remaining anonymous.

This book from Rohit Chawhan is a must read for all young people who are trying to survive, thrive and accomplish something in their life. The book through its emotional storyline conveys life s truths about love, passion, self-belief , perseverance, relationships, compassion, and success.

The protagonists are two young people with whom every young person can relate to and will empathise with their journey. They will know they are not alone. The book has takeaways and a positive message and a tool kit and formula to succeed and thrive.

The sheer authenticity of the book and the experiences recounted and the narrative makes the book unique and so relevant for current times.

The themes in each chapter are the themes and emotions young people are dealing with.

This book can help any young person transform and realise his or her dreams.

Reading the book is like watching a movie, it moves you and you experience the emotions Rohit wants you to feel and experience.

The storytelling is simple, without jargon and I will request every young entrepreneur and young aspirant of the Academy of life and success, must read this.

I will not be surprised if there are further sequels of this book and this is made into a major movie.

I wish Rohit and the readers of this book success.

let me end by saying This book proves " experience is what you get when you don't get what you want ".

Anurag Batra
Media Mogul, Entrepreneur, Author, TV show host, Angel investor and the man behind exchange4media and BW Business World groups

WORKSHEET

1. NOW MY DEAR READERS WRITE DOWN YOURS TOP TEN GOALS YOU WANT TO ACHIEVE IN NEXT 10 YEARS AND WRITE A REASON AFTER EVERY GOAL.

I. _____

II. _____

III. _____

IV. _____

V. _____

VI. _____

VII. _____

VIII._____

IX. _____

X. _____

2. NOW DEAR READERS IMAGINE AND WRITE DOWN YOUR COMMENCEMENT SPEECH WHICH YOU WILL GIVE AT THE MOST PRESTIGIOUS UNIVERSITY IN THE WORLD AFTER 20 YEARS.NOW REMEMBER WHAT YOU ARE WRITING THE SO CALLED GREAT SPEECH YOU SHOULD HAVE DONE WORK WORTH OF.SO ULTIMATELY WRITE THE SPEECH ON THE BASIS OF WHAT YOU WILL BE ACIEVING IN NEXT 20 YEARS AND ACCORDINLGY WORK ON IT TO MAKE IT HAPPEN IN REAL LIFE.

_____

_____

_____

_____

_____

_____

_____

_____

_____

_____

_____

_____

_____

3. STICK THE PAGE OR SAVE THE DOCUMENT IN WHICH WRITE AND SEE IT DAILY AND ASK YOURSELF ARE DOING WORK ACCORDINGLY SO THAT YOU CAN SAY IT IN YOUR FUTURE SPEECH.

4. HAVE HEROS AND IDEALS,ADMIRE THEM AND TRY TO LEARN THEIR HABITS AND ADAPT THEIR GOOD QUALITIES.

5. MAINTAIN A DIARY AND EVERYDAY BEFORE GOING TO BED WRITE WHAT I LEARNED TODAY.

6. MAKE A BUCKET LIST OF 100 THINGS YOU WANNA DO BEFORE YOU DIE AND WORK RELENTLESLY TO ACHIEVE IT.

DO THESE THINGS FOR SURE AND LOVE YOU ALL WHO ARE TRYING AND PUTTING GENUINE EFFORTS TO DO SOMETHING IN LIFE.

ROHIT CHAWHAN

About the Author

Rohit is A 17 YEARS OLD STUDENT WHO JUST FINISHED HIS SCHOOL AND HE IS CURRENTLY STUDYING IN CHRIST UNIVERSITY. He is unable to put himself in a particular slot but he knows that he is a crazy guy, crazy about money and fame. He never gets disheartened when he doesn't achieve what he has worked hard to get. He had a desire to write a story which also to some extent reflects his life and this book is the outcome.

He has been an above average throughout school. He never excelled in sports or extracurricular nor in forming close friendship with girls, though he has had great life experiences.

He HOPEs THIS STORY, WHEN PEOPLE READ it WIL MAKE him,and all those important to him proud that he is from DPS DURG, A TOWN IN CHHATTISGARH KNOWN AS BHILAI.